Walt Disney's
PINOCCHIO

PICTURES BY THE WALT DISNEY STUDIO

ADAPTED BY AL DEMPSTER

Story Adapted by Steffi Fletcher from the Motion Picture "Pinocchio"

BASED ON THE STORY BY COLLODI

gb **GOLDEN PRESS**
Western Publishing Company, Inc.
Racine, Wisconsin

Twenty-Eighth Printing, 1976

ISBN 0-307-10580-6   ISBN 0-307-60580-9   (lib. bdg.)

NE NIGHT, long, long ago, the Evening Star shone down across the dark sky. Its beams formed a shimmering pathway to a tiny village, whose humble little homes lay deep in sleep. Only one house still had a light burning in the window, and that was the workshop of Geppetto, the kindly old woodcarver.

Geppetto had stayed up to finish a merry-faced little puppet he was carving. Now he held the puppet up. "Look, Figaro! Look, Cleo!" he chuckled. "Isn't Pinocchio almost like a real boy?"

The only answer was a snore. Figaro had his soft kitten nose folded into his paws, and Cleo lay sleeping in her goldfish bowl.

"Sleepy-heads!" the old woodcarver sighed. Climbing creakily into bed, he mumbled, "I wish you really were a real boy, Pinocchio!"

Somebody overheard Geppetto's wish, and that was Cricket, Jiminy Cricket. All evening Jiminy had sat hidden behind the hearth. He had seen how kind and gentle the woodcarver was, and he felt sorry because he knew the lonely old man's wish could never come true.

Suddenly a shimmering light filled the room. Jiminy gasped. Out of the light stepped a beautiful lady dressed in shining blue. She raised her wand and said:

"Wake, Pinocchio! Skip and run! Good Geppetto needs a son!"

Pinocchio blinked his eyes and raised his wooden arms.

"I can move!" he cried. "I'm a real boy!"

"No," the Blue Fairy said sadly. "You have life, but to become a real boy, you must prove yourself brave, truthful, and unselfish."

"But how can I do that?" asked Pinocchio, discouraged.

"You'll have a Conscience to help you!" Looking around, the Blue Fairy beckoned Jiminy out of his hiding place. "*Sir* Jiminy Cricket," she said, "I dub you Lord High Keeper of Pinocchio's Conscience!"

The next morning Geppetto couldn't stop rubbing his eyes. There was the puppet he had carved last night, laughing and chattering and running around the workshop!

"No, no, it can't be true!" Geppetto argued. "It's a dream!"

But Pinocchio ran to him and threw his wooden arms around his neck. "It's true, Father!" he cried. "It's true! I'm alive!"

And then Geppetto realized that a miracle had really happened.

After his first great joy was over, Geppetto said, "But now, Pinocchio, you must go to school." He brought out a bundle of school books. "Study hard! Then you'll soon become a real boy!"

Pinocchio nodded happily. "Good-by, Father!" he shouted, and off he marched, his books under his arm, chockful of good resolutions.

Meanwhile, Jiminy Cricket had overslept and now jumped up in a great hurry. Quickly he stuffed his shirt into his trousers and rushed out. "Hey, Pinoke!" he called. "Wait for me!"

Panting, he caught up with Pinocchio just as the silly little puppet was walking off arm in arm with the worst pair of scoundrels in the whole countryside! The villains were a Fox by the name of J. Worthington Foulfellow, and a stupid Cat called Gideon.

"Yes," the sly Fox was saying to Pinocchio, "you're too talented a boy to waste your time in school, isn't he, Gideon?"

Gideon nodded.

"With that face, you should be an actor, my boy!"

Pinocchio smiled, pleased at the flattery.

"But, Pinoke!" cried Jiminy. "What will your father say!"

Pinocchio looked startled when he saw Jiminy. He said crossly, "Oh, Father will be proud of me!"

Jiminy knew Pinocchio was being foolish. But the Blue Fairy had appointed him the puppet's Conscience, so he followed along loyally.

Soon they came to a marionette theater. When Stromboli, its owner, saw Pinocchio, his small evil eyes glistened. "What a drawing card!" he breathed. "A puppet without strings!"

The Fox nodded. "And he's yours," he said, smiling greedily and holding out his paw, "for a certain price, of course!"

That night Pinocchio sang and danced with the spotlight upon him, as Foulfellow had promised. The audience clapped and cheered and roared for more. A puppet without strings! It was a miracle!

Jiminy, sitting in the audience, felt terrible. "You'd better congratulate Pinocchio and go off . . . alone," he thought sadly to himself. "What does a great actor need a Conscience for?"

After the show, Pinocchio held out his hand to Stromboli and said shyly, "Good-by, sir, and thank you. Shall I come back tomorrow?"

Stromboli smiled an ugly smile. "Not so fast, young man," he snarled. "You're mine, and you stay here!" And bang! before Pinocchio could resist, he was locked in a birdcage!

Suddenly the Blue Fairy stood before them! She asked, "Pinocchio, why didn't you go to school?"

"School? Well, I ... uh ..." Pinocchio began. "I *was* going to school till I met somebody."

"Met somebody?"

"Yeah! Uh ... two big monsters!"

Jiminy clapped both hands to his head and frowned. Pinocchio's nose began to grow longer.

"Monsters?" asked the Blue Fairy. "Weren't you afraid?"

"No, ma'am," said Pinocchio. "But they tied me in a big sack!"

His nose grew even longer. He squinted at it in surprise. "Oh, my nose!   What's happened?"

The Blue Fairy said, "Perhaps you haven't been telling the truth, Pinocchio. You see, a lie keeps growing and growing, until it's as plain as the nose on your face."

Pinocchio was ashamed. "I'll never lie again — honest, I won't."

"Very well," said the Blue Fairy. "I'll help you this time, because you are truly sorry. Be good now, Pinocchio."

And as she waved her wand, Jiminy and Pinocchio found themselves standing on the open road again!

"Whew!" Pinocchio sighed thankfully. "Let's go home, Jiminy!"

The two friends started running as fast as they could, when whom should they bump into but Foulfellow and Gideon!

"Pinocchio!" Foulfellow cried. "My dearest young friend! How does it feel to be a great actor?"

"Awful!" said Pinocchio. "Stromboli put me in a cage!" And he told Foulfellow how badly he had fared.

The sly Fox pretended to be deeply shocked. Before Jiminy knew what had happened, Foulfellow had persuaded the gullible puppet to forget his good resolutions and take a "rest cure" on Pleasure Island.

"Pinocchio!" Jiminy cried. "You promised to go right home!"

"I will, Jiminy, later on! But Foulfellow says I need a rest after my terrible experience. Just think of Pleasure Island—bands, circuses, ice-cream mountains!"

They came to a coach bound for Pleasure Island. It was pulled by small donkeys and filled with impudent, noisy boys. As Pinocchio climbed eagerly aboard, Jiminy saw the evil-looking Coachman slip Foulfellow a heavy bag. Again the Fox had sold Pinocchio!

The Coachman whirled his whip, the boys shouted, and the coach started. The only ones who didn't seem happy were Jiminy and the small donkeys, but no one paid any attention to them.

After having boarded a ferry, the coach and its noisy passengers docked at Pleasure Island. Down the gangplank piled the boys. Here were bands playing, streets paved with cookies and lined with dough-nut trees, and fountains spouting lemonade. And always the Coachman kept urging the boys, "Have a good time—while you can!"

And they did! They climbed the Ice-cream Mountains and sailed down the Lemonade River. They smashed windows, burned school-books, and teased the poor little donkeys. Pinocchio made friends with the very worst of the boys, a young bully called Lampwick, and he was always in the middle of the mischief.

One day, down in Tobacco Lane, Jiminy came upon Pinocchio puffing on a corncob pipe. Lampwick had a big cigar. Jiminy lost his temper and shook his little fist angrily. "This has gone far enough!" he shouted. "Throw away that pipe! Come home this minute!"

Pinocchio looked sheepish, but Lampwick began to snicker.

"Don't tell me you're scared of a *beetle!*" he said insultingly.

The puppet hesitated a minute. Then he said quickly, "Gosh, no, Lampwick. That's only Jiminy. He can't tell me anything!" And right in Jiminy's face, he blew a puff of smoke!

Jiminy was about to march off angrily when suddenly Lampwick grabbed his head, and Pinocchio groaned, "Jiminy, my ears buzz!"

Before Jiminy's shocked eyes, the boys were sprouting donkey ears!

"It's donkey fever!" whispered Jiminy, horrified. "You were lazy, good-for-nothing boys, so you're turning into donkeys. Let's get out of here!"

This time no one argued with the cricket. As fast as they could, they dashed through the strangely deserted streets.

As they rounded a corner, they came face to face with the Coach-man. He and armed guards were herding a bunch of braying, howling donkeys, many of which still wore boys' hats and shoes.

"There they go! That's the two that's missing!" yelled the Coachman. "After them!"

Bullets whizzed past them as they rushed toward the wall surrounding the island. Pinocchio and Jiminy managed to clamber up, but when they looked down, they saw a little donkey in Lampwick's clothes. It was Lampwick.

"Go on, Pinoke!" he cried. "It's all up with me!"

There was nothing they could do. With a lump in his throat, Pinocchio followed Jiminy and dove into the sea.

They had a long, hard swim to the mainland, and a longer, harder journey home. It was winter when they came to the village. Through the drifting snow they hurried to Geppetto's door and pounded on it.

The only answer was the howling of the wintry wind. Worried, Pinocchio peered into the window. The house was empty!

"My father's gone away!" said Pinocchio, and a tear ran down his long nose and froze into a tiny, sparkling icicle.

Just then a gust of wind blew a piece of paper around the corner. "Hey, Pinoke!" Jiminy exclaimed. "It's a letter!"

The little cricket began to read the note aloud:

"Dear Pinocchio:

"I heard you had gone to Pleasure Island, so Figaro, Cleo and I started off in a small boat to find you. Just as we came in sight of the island, out of the sea rose Monstro, the giant whale. He opened his jaws; in we went. Now, dear son, we are living in the belly of the whale. But there is very little to eat here, and we cannot exist much longer, so I fear you will never again see

"Your loving father,

"GEPPETTO."

For a while, both Jiminy and Pinocchio were silent, too heavy-hearted to speak. Then Pinocchio said in a resolute voice that Jiminy had never heard him use before, "I am going to save my father!"

"But Pinocchio," cried Jiminy, "think how far it is to the ocean!"

"I don't mind," Pinocchio said firmly. "I must find Father."

Just then a soft voice said, "I will take you," and out of the sky fluttered a small white dove, with a golden crown on its head.

Pinocchio stared. "You?" he asked. "How could you carry us?"

"Like this!" And the dove began to grow and grow. "Climb on," she commanded, and, spreading her wings, flew off. All day and all night they flew, until they reached the high cliffs of the seashore.

They landed. "Good-by!" called the dove. "Good luck!" And she flew away. They did not know that she was their own Blue Fairy in disguise, and that it was she who had brought them Geppetto's letter.

When the dove was out of sight, Pinocchio tied a big stone to his donkey tail. He smiled bravely at Jiminy, and together they leaped off the cliff into the roaring ocean below.

Down, down, down they went, through the green water, past clumps of waving seaweed. As soon as they reached the sandy bottom, Pinocchio scrambled to his feet. "Come on," he said. "Let's find Monstro." He started off, peering into every grotto and green sea cave.

"We'll never find him," muttered Jiminy. "We're probably looking in the wrong ocean!"

Jiminy was wrong. Very near them floated the whale they were looking for, fast asleep. Inside the whale, at the far end of his mouth's dark cavern, Geppetto had set up a strange household. He had salvaged a rude home from ships the whale had swallowed, and every day he fished in the whale's mouth. But now that Monstro was sleeping, no fish came in.

"Not a bite for days, Figaro," Geppetto said mournfully. "If Monstro doesn't wake soon, we'll all starve."

It was a solemn moment. All felt that the end was near.

And then the whale moved!

Monstro gave an upward lunge, and through his jaw rushed a wall of black water. With it came fish—a whole school of tuna!

Near by, Pinocchio saw the sea creatures fleeing. He had a glimpse of Monstro coming at him. Then he, too, was sucked down that huge maw.

Only Jiminy was left outside. Bobbing up and down on an empty bottle, he begged to be swallowed too. But Monstro just went back to sleep.

Meanwhile, Geppetto was pulling fish after fish out of the water. "Food!" he yelled. "Oh, Figaro, Cleo—we are saved!"

He was so busy, he scarcely heard a shrill cry of "Father!"

"Pinocchio?" he asked wonderingly, and turned around. "Oh, my own dear son!" he exclaimed. "Is it really you?"

With tears in his eyes the old man embraced Pinocchio. But when he lovingly took off his son's hat, out popped the hated donkey ears.

Pinocchio turned his face away in shame. "I've got a tail, too," he admitted sadly. "Oh, Father!"

"Never mind, son," Geppetto said comfortingly. "The main thing is that we are all together again."

"And that we get out of here," Pinocchio added.

"We never will. I've tried everything . . . even built a raft . . ."

"That's it!" cried Pinocchio. "When Monstro opens his mouth, we'll float out on the raft."

"Oh, no," argued Geppetto. "When Monstro opens his mouth, everything comes in—nothing comes out."

"Yes," said Pinocchio thoughtfully, "if he swallows. But not . . . not if he sneezes! Quick, Father, help me build a fire!"

Before Geppetto knew what he was doing, Pinocchio set fire to a pile of chairs and crates he had quickly tossed together.

As the fire began to smoke, they got the raft ready. The whale began to grunt. Suddenly he drew in his breath and gave a monstrous SNEEZE!

Out went the raft, past those crushing jaws, into the open sea!

But they were not yet free. The angry whale saw them and plunged after them. With one blow he splintered their frail craft.

Geppetto felt himself sinking. "My son, save yourself!" he cried.

But the brave puppet swam to him and kept him afloat. Giant waves swept them toward dark rocks looming against the shore. Just as they were about to be crushed against the rocks, they were washed through a tiny crevice into a lagoon. In vain did Monstro hurl his bulk against the other side. His prey had escaped!

Geppetto lay on the beach, gratitude filling his heart. And then he saw Pinocchio lying beside him, still, cold and pale!